BEADS of COURAGE®

(OLIVER'S STORY)

ROSANNA GARTLEY

A Mouse Gate Adventure™

Mouse Gate Press
1103 Middlecreek
Friendswood, Texas 77546
281-992-3131 TEL
www.mousegate.com

Copyright © 2017 by: Rosanna Gartley
All rights reserved
Edited by: Sigrid Macdonald
Cover photo by Raeanne Muir

ISBN: 978-1-59095-226-9
UPC: 6-43977-62260 0

Library of Congress Control Number: 2017949658

Printed in the United States of America with simultaneous printings in Australia, Canada, and the United Kingdom.

FIRST EDITION
1   2   3   4   5   6   7   8   9   10

Dedicated to my beautiful grandson, Oliver,
and his family, with whom I had the privilege
of sharing their experience.

Dedicated to those who need a bead for
courage, which is all of us.

–Grandma Rosie

Acknowledgments

Thank you to my husband, John, for his support in so many ways. Thanks to my publisher, Mouse Gate Press, Inc., my editor, Sigrid Macdonald, Raeanne Muir for photographing Oliver's beads for the cover and those who encouraged me to continue with this project. Thanks, also, to Beads of Courage® for doing what you do.

The Book

Baby Oliver's life started out precariously in the neonatal intensive care unit. Each day, while he was a patient, his parents were given beads of various shapes and colors. Each bead symbolized a medical procedure that Oliver had endured on that day. By the time Oliver was discharged, his collection of beads was impressive.

As Oliver grew, his Beads of Courage® continued to hang on his bedroom wall. Not only were they a reminder of what he had lived through but also served as an inspiration for future challenges.

You won't want to miss what happens during a family vacation when this amazing little boy employs Disney magic to help those who need a little courage.

Beads of Courage® Mission Statement

The mission of Beads of Courage, Inc.(a 501(c)3 tax-exempt organization) is to provide innovative arts-in-medicine programs for children coping with serious illness, their families, and the clinicians who care for them.

Through Beads of Courage® we help children Record, Tell and Own their Story of Courage. Through the Beads of Courage® Program, children receive colorful beads that symbolize each step of their treatment journey. The beads they receive provide a powerful dose of narrative medicine that visually translates their treatment experience and helps them cope with the many uncertainties of their treatment journey. Every bead makes visible the otherwise invisible. Beads of Courage® serve as metaphors that help the child derive meaning from their experience, and help them connect to others in their life that might otherwise never comprehend all that they have been through.

From research, we know that the Beads of Courage® Program makes children who participate happy, provides a new coping strategy that helps them get through the day to day treatments, and restores their confidence and self-worth helping them stand strong and be proud of what they accomplish while receiving treatment for a serious illness.

Beads of Courage® Programs currently support more than 250 participating member hospitals in the United States, Japan, New Zealand, Canada and the United Kingdom.

To learn more please visit:
www.beadsofcourage.org

"There is something you must
always remember.

You are braver than you believe,
stronger than you seem, and smarter
than you think."

--Winnie the Pooh©

Chapter 1

It all started before the baby's birth. His inner calendar told him he still had several more weeks of nurturing before he would be mature enough to be born, so he snuggled down inside his mother, both protected yet vulnerable, at the same time. Today, the usual, familiar noises surrounded him, the ones he had come to recognize as he grew. For several months now, he had been able to recognize his mother's voice. He could also tell when his daddy spoke and when his brother and sister argued. He had learned to tell the difference between the voices of visitors and those on the television, and he could even associate some sounds with movement. A loud humming noise was accompanied by his mom swaying back and forth. Eventually, he would learn that was called vacuuming. The swishing sound of the dishwasher and the country music wafting from the kitchen radio were soothing sounds the baby heard daily.

When he heard the familiar start of an engine and felt the gentle bouncing of his mother, Oliver was lulled to sleep. After a long nap, the bouncing stopped, and he realized they were in a familiar place—the doctor's office. He was used to this, too. Someone's hands would soon be pressing on him, there would be a conversation, and then they would leave. Today, he could hear his parents talking with the doctor for a long time, and instead of starting the two-hour car ride home, the journey was short. As they talked in the car, his parent's voices sounded excited yet worried.

It wasn't long before the infant noticed changes around him. Every once in a while, it felt as though someone were squeezing him from inside his mother. He tried to sleep, but the squeezing became more frequent. Then he felt pressure pushing him down, head first. Soon the top of his head was feeling cold. It was uncomfortable, but there was no stopping his descent. Next, bright lights shone into his eyes making it impossible to keep them open. He felt scared, cold, vulnerable, as well as confused, and let out a loud cry to let the world know it.

"It's a boy!" someone said as he was hoisted up into the air. An object was pushed into his nose and mouth. Then he was laid on top of his mother. He recognized her smell and felt safer now, but almost before she could cuddle him, he was whisked away to be weighed. He was too small and was taken to the neonatal intensive care unit (NICU) for monitoring. He was frightened, almost to the point of being in shock. Too much had changed within the past hour. Where was his mommy, and why couldn't he hear his daddy's reassuring voice? Who were these people handling him? He had never felt pain before, but now his heels were being poked, and blood was drawn from him. He wanted to scream, but he was so tired that only a whimper escaped from his pale lips.

Meanwhile, his mom and dad were scared, too. This was not how the birth of their son was supposed to play out. Blood draw reports revealed the baby wasn't able to stabilize a safe level of sugar in his blood. His blood sugar kept dropping, so they poked him again and started giving him sugar water through a tiny tube placed into a vein. Everyone hoped that once the baby began drinking his mother's milk, the problem would take care of itself. But until that happened, he would stay in the NICU.

Now that a plan for the baby had been

decided, his parents focused on a name. If their baby was a boy, they had decided to call him Oliver Cruz; so Oliver it was! Although Oliver was light in weight, he was beautiful. His most striking features were his long arms and legs, taking after his Grandpa Bruce. He had big eyes and a perfectly shaped head that was crowned with dark hair. He looked a lot like his big brother, Cooper.

Every day, Oliver's mom and dad came to the NICU to hold, feed and get to know their new son. They listened intently as the medical team made daily rounds focusing their attention on newborn Oliver. Every day, blood tests indicated a drop in his blood sugar despite his ability to drink breast milk plus the higher doses of sugar water he was being given. It looked like Oliver would be in the NICU longer than anyone expected. One morning, his nurse thought he looked pale and mentioned her observation to Oliver's doctor. It turned out that they had done so many blood draws for testing purposes that he had become anemic. That was when he needed his first blood transfusion.

Oliver's health took a serious turn. The medical team diagnosed him with an infection and hoped it was of the staph variety commonly found in hospitals. But it wasn't. The team began to worry that it might be meningitis, a very serious illness that is a known killer especially for someone as fragile as a newborn baby. A spinal tap was necessary to determine a diagnosis. Fortunately, Oliver did not have meningitis, but the infection he was suffering from remained a mystery. The medical team began to give him multiple types of antibiotics to kill whatever was attacking his system.

The infection and the drugs took their toll on Oliver. His body needed all of its energy to fight off the infection, so the doctors put Oliver to sleep, attaching him to a breathing machine, and inserting a feeding tube so he would not have to use any of his own energy to breathe or eat. The uncertainty of his future left his parents terrified as there was no hiding the seriousness of his condition. To make matters worse, they could not hold or touch him. The less stimulation he had, the more his body could rest. All they could do was sit by his tiny bed and watch the monitor screens display his vital signs and wince whenever an alarm went off. They cringed when they saw all the tubes and wires attached to their helpless baby, but Oliver's nurses handled him lovingly despite all the hardware. They spoke gently to him while they changed him and repositioned him, forever keeping an eye on his monitors. But his mommy and daddy could only sit and watch, comforting each other while praying that their little miracle would be strong enough to continue fighting.

It was during this nightmare that a curious ritual started. Each day, a nurse would read through Oliver's medical chart and tally the number and types of procedures he had endured that day. Each procedure matched a certain shape and color of bead, and every day, Oliver's parents were given those beads to put into a little bag. The nurse called them Beads of Courage®.

Chapter 2

The mix of antibiotics, love, and prayers worked, and almost a month after his birth, Oliver was able to go home. He was still very small, and the preemie sized clothes he was dressed in were too big. Despite his precarious start in life, once home, Oliver grew in size and strength. The days, weeks, and months went by quickly, as they always do. Eventually, Oliver became a rough and tumble boy who idolized his sister and brother. He had grown slightly taller than most boys his age, his arms and legs still seemingly too gangly for his body. He was truly a mix of his parents. His big blue eyes, goofy-looking feet, and head of curls came from his dad, but his olive complexion and dark brown hair favored his mother. The only reminders of his neonatal illness were the memories and Beads of Courage® hanging on Oliver's wall. He had always been told that his string of beads meant he could handle anything that came his way, no matter how frightening. They were proof of his bravery.

People referred to Oliver's beads often. His first time on skates was daunting for the two-year-old. He was excited to learn to skate until Daddy tied his skates on and he tried to walk in them. The ice looked very hard and slippery. His sister, Dylan, and brother, Cooper, had already mastered hockey, and despite their urgings, all Oliver would do was look at the ice with tears in his eyes. Daddy could see the hesitation and fear in his little boy's eyes, and he said, "Oliver, remember your beads. You can do this."

My beads, thought Oliver. *I can do this.* He stepped out on the ice and immediately landed on his bum. Without hesitation, he let Daddy help him up, and by the end of the hour, he could slowly move across the ice all by himself.

The next major hurdle for Oliver was going to school. He had watched Dylan and Cooper run to the school bus each morning then hop off the bus at the end of the lane each afternoon. He wanted to go, too. But when the morning came for his first ride on that school bus, he wasn't so sure. After breakfast, he had dressed himself in his new blue jeans and superhero t-shirt. His new red running shoes fit perfectly, and his yellow and black backpack made him look like a big boy. Yet, all of a sudden, he didn't want to take Dylan's hand and walk to the end of the lane. He wanted to stay home with Mommy.

Mommy knew her little boy well, and as she watched a tear slide down Oliver's cheek, she bent down and put her arms around him. "What's wrong, sweetheart?"

"I'm scared," he whispered into her ear, not wanting anyone else to hear.

"That's okay," assured his mom. "Dylan and Cooper were scared to start school, too."

"They were?"

"Yes, they were, although I doubt they would admit it," smiled Mom. "It's all going to work out fine, Oliver. Remember your beads."

"I forgot," said Oliver.

"Your beads will be here waiting for you when you get off the bus. Daddy and I can't wait to hear about all the exciting things you'll do today in Miss Connor's class." Oliver wiped his tears away and blew his nose into the tissue his mom held out for him. He could picture his beads on the wall, and he hoped today would be okay. And it was.

Each year slipped quietly into the next, and somehow eight years had passed since Oliver had come home for the first time. Christmas was just around the corner, and the house was full of excitement. The Christmas tree was up, and a few wrapped gifts had found their way beneath it. Oliver's favorite part of the day was when Mommy and Daddy would snuggle the kids around them and read their bedtime story by the lights of the tree.

One more sleep and everyone would be able to open their presents. It was hard for Oliver to fall asleep, but before he knew it, big brother Cooper was shaking him awake.

"Get up, Oliver. I think Santa came!" It took Oliver only half of a second to remember that today was Christmas. By the time he jumped out of bed, he could hear Dylan waking up Mommy and Daddy. The whole family started down the stairs toward the living room. Daddy walked to the kitchen to turn on the coffee pot while Mommy tied her pink robe around her waist and then reached behind the tree to turn on the pretty lights.

"Let's start with our stockings," suggested Mommy as she began removing them from the mantle. They were filled to the brim, and Oliver and his siblings could hardly wait to dump out their contents. Each received some cool socks, an orange, peanut butter and cracker packs, candy and chocolate. Dylan also got some pink, smelly lip stuff that neither brother was interested in. As soon as Daddy appeared with coffee for himself and Mom, the kids knew that was their cue to dive into the present pile. With excitement fueling the children, it didn't take long for the mound of gifts to be transformed into three distinct piles of new toys and clothes. Mom and Dad began picking up the torn wrapping paper and stuffing it into black garbage bags, being cautious not to discard any new treasures by mistake. Dylan was busy admiring her new clothes like girls do, and Cooper was trying on his new hockey skates. Oliver was intrigued by a new video game he had received from Santa when Dad walked up to the tree. As Oliver looked up, he saw his dad reach for something that was near the tippy top.

"What's up there, Dad?" asked Cooper.

"I think there might be a gift that we missed."

Dylan quit examining a new dress and said, "Who's it for?"

"Let's read it and see," he replied. All the children crowded around their dad as he plucked the white envelope that was poking out from between the branches. Just then, Mom came back into the room, and as Dad began to open it, he glanced at her, slyly winking.

What could it be? Oliver wondered. Pages were pulled out of the envelope, and a couple of quick glimpses of the pictures on those papers gave Oliver some big clues. He saw a castle and black mouse ears. That could only mean one thing— Disney World. Sure enough! As Dad held up the photos for everyone to see, there were squeals, laughter, clapping, dancing, hopping, jumping and pure joy.

"When are we going?" screeched Dylan.

"I need my suitcase," announced Cooper.

"What should I pack?" asked Dylan.

"Whoa, whoa, everybody. You'll have plenty of time to pack. We don't leave for about six weeks. We'll go during your winter break, so you don't have to miss much school," said Mom sensibly. Each night before bed, the children took turns marking that day off on the calendar with a big black X. Before they knew it, there were only a few days left that weren't crossed off. One day after school, once the kids ran through the snow drifts in the lane leading up to the house, breathless with pink cheeks and runny noses, they saw their suitcases upstairs in their bedrooms. This gesture added another level of excitement!

Just seeing the suitcase in his room made Oliver so psyched, he could hardly stand it. Mommy had made it clear that each night she would help one child pack. Oliver's turn wasn't until tomorrow. He just didn't know how he was expected ever to fall asleep tonight!

Finally, the last day of school and the last hockey practice came and went before the family's big trip. Everyone was packed, the house had been cleaned, the SUV was all gassed up, and now they were all tucked in their beds; excitement was running high. Tomorrow, they would drive to the city and spend some time with their aunt and uncle before going to the airport.

Chapter 3

At last, Oliver and his family were at Disney World. They had flown into Orlando, Florida, a few hours earlier and were now gathered on Mom and Dad's hotel room bed trying to figure out what they would do in the morning. After looking at maps and the park's brochure, they devised a hodge-podge kind of itinerary for the next day. They would spend much of the next day on the rides. Oliver thought some of them looked scary, but he wasn't about to say anything 'cause he knew Cooper would tease him. It had been a long and exciting day. The whole family began to yawn and despite the new adventures planned for the morning, everyone was asleep minutes after being tucked in.

Bright, beautiful Florida sunshine flooded their rooms the next morning. No one had to wake up the children; they were eager to dress, eat, and get going! They stepped outside the hotel on the way to their rented SUV when the kids began to yell and point. For the first time, they saw a real palm tree.

"Can we eat coconuts from them?" asked Cooper.

"Not all palm trees produce coconuts," explained Dad. "But we will see if we can get all of you your own coconuts later."

Wow, thought Oliver. *This place really is magical!*

By the time they had reached the park, they had experienced many firsts. They had seen more palm trees than they could have imagined. They felt the warm sun and humidity in the middle of winter, unlike home where there was only ice and snow. Surprisingly, some people had on warm parkas and mitts, yet they were comfortable wearing shorts! The monorail had been amazing, and then they stepped foot for the first time in Disney World! There was so much to see, Oliver couldn't swivel his head around fast enough.

The entrance to the park led them onto Main Street, USA. It was set up like a real town from the early 1900s. Not only were there many old-fashioned buildings and stores, but each of them was real! Visitors could go inside them all and buy stuff. Beyond Main Street, far in the distance, was Cinderella's castle. He had seen it on TV many times and here it was. It was huge, it was grand, and Oliver wanted to get to it and go inside.

"Whoa there, Oliver," said Mom as Oliver pulled her toward the castle. "We will get there. One thing at a time. We don't want to miss all of this," she said, pointing out the many buildings flanking them on both sides. "Besides," she continued, "We need to get to where some of the Disney characters are if you want to meet them and have your picture taken."

"Okay," said Oliver, remembering he wanted to meet Mickey Mouse and some of the others. Of course, there were still the rides. The family had made a ride list the night before, and Oliver was excited about getting on most of them. The only one he was really worried about was Splash Mountain. It looked very high, very fast, and very dark. Oliver put it out of his mind; there were many other things to do before he would have to stand in line for the big, scary roller coaster.

It was past lunchtime when the family took a break. They found some outdoor tables, and after a quick lunch of hot dogs, fries, and drinks, it was time to go to Splash Mountain. Cooper and Dylan ran ahead, eager to get a place in line. Oliver hung back, holding tightly onto Daddy's hand. He had seen the roller coaster on television. He knew how the ride ended—splashing through a large puddle and getting wet while a camera took a picture. Most of the children he saw were screaming with delight; some weren't even holding on, instead raising their arms above their heads. The closer they walked to the mountain, the higher it seemed. While in line, he watched many children finish the ride with their coaster car sailing straight down or so it seemed! How would he ever be able to do this?

Slowly, they moved toward the front of the line. Mommy stood with Cooper and Dylan in front of Oliver and Daddy. As he watched them get into their car, Oliver's stomach flipped. He knew they were next.

"Ready, sport?" asked Daddy as an empty car stopped in front of them.

"No, Dad, I don't want to go," pleaded Oliver.

"I know it looks scary, but I promise you will love it." Daddy looked down and saw tears in Oliver's eyes. "Remember your beads."

"Okay," said Oliver as a tear escaped onto his cheek, and he held Daddy's hand even tighter. The two were strapped in; then the car moved slowly up and up into the mountain. Darker and darker it became, and Oliver closed his eyes, not wanting to see what was coming next. Then a magical thing happened. When he opened his eyes, he was no longer in Disney World.

Oliver's sense of smell took over while his eyes were closed. The odors were ones he recognized, almost comforting, so when his eyes opened, he wasn't surprised to find himself inside a hospital. He wasn't scared for he knew why he was there. The hospital would provide many opportunities for him to help others, and he knew the connection to this adventure were his Beads of Courage®.

Chapter 4

Never having been in this particular hospital before, Oliver relied on his intuition to find his way to the NICU. He was sure he must be invisible for no one would allow a little boy to wander around a hospital, especially giving him access to a very sensitive area that cared for sick newborns. Oliver slipped into the unit and stood close to the nurses' desk. He was instantly reminded of the sounds, smells, and sights that had surrounded him years ago. The memories brought up mixed feelings from when he was an infant. While he had been a patient, he had ached to have his mommy's arms around him, to hear the comforting sound of her heartbeat as well as feel his daddy's strong and loving touch. It also reminded him of the dedication and heartfelt concern he had received from the doctors and nurses who had cared for him, which had ended with his ability to go home.

Once he became accustomed to the layout of

the place, he moved away from the desk and walked toward an incubator near the back wall. The pink tag taped to the outside of the plastic case protecting the infant said 'Catherine.' He didn't need to see her chart to know her story. She had been born only a couple of hours ago, early by several months. She wasn't exactly sick, just very small. Oliver could tell that although there was concern, no one, not even Catherine's parents, was frightened. It would only be a matter of time before their daughter would finish growing in the NICU instead of inside her mother. Once she gained some weight, she would go home.

The next bassinet held a much sicker baby and was positioned closer to the nurses station. The little boy, named Kelly, had been born with serious asthma. His lungs were not healthy, and he relied on a machine to breathe for him. He had already been in the NICU for two months and only recently had shown small signs of improvement. His family had been extremely worried about his survival. They had prayed daily, and now there were signs that the medication was working.

Oliver looked up from the baby. He recognized the sounds of his monitor and felt oddly comforted by the beeping it made, the sight of the gloved nurses and the tiny tubes weaving their way in and out of the bassinet. Not only did Oliver recognize what the tubes were for, he knew how they felt. Although Kelly wasn't as healthy as he was going to be, Oliver knew he would be going home soon.

Oliver's attention became focused on the baby in the first bed. Now he knew why he had been drawn to the NICU; this baby needed courage. His parents, Emma and Jack, sat vigil at his bedside, holding each other's hands. The baby lay silent with a tiny diaper between his legs, multiple tubes, and wires monitoring his every function, ear muffs over his ears to keep out the monotonous sounds around him, and his eyes tightly closed. He had been given medication to keep him sleeping while a machine did all his breathing for him.

He had been a miracle from conception and his parents prayed that nothing would change. They had married over a decade ago and had begun trying to get pregnant a few years into their marriage. When they did not conceive, both tested for infertility. They had become frustrated when doctors could not discover any reason for their inability to become pregnant. It was then that they turned to adoption. They were thrilled when a newborn baby had been found for them, and while paperwork and bureaucracy slowed down the process, eventually they were handed a two-month-old baby boy whom they named Jeffrey.

Six months ago, Emma began to feel sick. She had all the symptoms of the flu, and day after day lay on the couch with nausea and no energy. When, after several weeks, she did not improve, she visited her medical provider. The first thing the nurse practitioner did was order a pregnancy test, much to Emma's objections. Sure enough, it came back positive! They were going to have a baby! She couldn't wait to share the news with Jack—this was indeed a miracle. The pregnancy continued as it should until the twenty-four-week mark when suddenly Emma went into labor. Despite their best efforts, the medical team was unable to stop the contractions, and a tiny boy had been born about three months premature. He weighed less than three pounds with underdeveloped organs. He would need much medical attention to survive. This had all happened within the past few hours. Jack and Emma were still in disbelief about the unscheduled birth of their son, and the tiny baby was in shock from the much too early delivery. His name was Jaxson, and he was very, very scared.

Oliver looked at the monitor that showed Jaxson's heart rate was much too high while his blood pressure was too low. Oliver reasoned that if Jaxson could relax a little maybe, his vital signs would improve. Courage is what he needed. The courage to accept his new environment and have faith in those who were caring for him. Silently, Oliver reached for a bead from his pocket and placed it near the baby's bed. The green bead began to glow, faintly at first, then its radiance blanketed the newborn with its gift.

Having done all he could do, Oliver backed away from Jaxson's little bed. He looked up into the faces of Jaxson's nurses and was reminded with fondness of the nurses who had cared for him. He remembered how they used to begin each shift with a prayer spoken aloud asking God to bless the babies they would care for, and for God to grant them the wisdom, patience, competence and compassion that they would need to care for the critically ill babies and their families. Oliver knew that Catherine, Kelly, and Jaxson would know the touch of deeply caring individuals during their hospital journey.

Oliver's mission in the NICU was complete but he felt he wouldn't be leaving the hospital just yet. There were others that needed his help. He left the babies and made his way to the bank of elevators.

Chapter 5

The elevator doors opened, and Oliver stepped in along with a doctor, nurse, and two visitors. After climbing for a few seconds, the elevator stopped before its doors opened onto the oncology floor. Quizzical glances bounced back and forth between the elevator's other occupants since none of them had pushed the sixth floor button.

This part of the hospital was new to Oliver, but strangely he knew where he needed to go. He paused at the doorway of a room halfway down a long, light blue hallway. The door was open a couple of inches, and when he went in, he couldn't see a thing. The room was very dark. All of the lights were turned off, and the heavy drapes were pulled shut. The first thing Oliver noticed were the red and green displays on the various monitors that blinked continuously. Bags of fluid hung on both sides of the bed, and he could see the patient's central line peeking out from above the top left side of the blue hospital gown. Oliver placed some sanitizer from the wall dispenser into his hands. Because he was invisible, he didn't know if that was necessary, but he had first-hand knowledge of how dangerous germs could be, and he was determined not to be the cause of anyone's suffering.

He turned his attention to the figure lying in the bed. It was sixteen-year-old Nick. He had been battling cancer for more than four years. Oliver looked reverently at the young man and thought how Nick could be a poster child for cancer. He lay still with the head of the bed raised, his sunken eyes closed. He had no hair left on his head, and if Oliver had leaned in closer, he would have seen that the patient's eyelashes and eyebrows were gone, too. The hospital room décor proved Nick had been here for some time. The wall opposite the bed was plastered in greeting cards sent by friends, relatives, and classmates. Half a dozen tired Mylar balloons hung in limbo in a tangled web by the window while a zoo of stuffed animals lined the shelving near the television.

Instead of the usual cotton blanket at the foot of Nick's bed, there was a carefully folded, handmade quilt. A white ceramic mug decorated with the gold and black colors of his high school was perched on the over-bed table alongside a video game controller. A rather large smartphone lay on Nick's bed while his laptop took up the bedside table top. On the other side of the room under a chair sat Nick's book bag. The textbooks and class assignments it held encouraged the charade that it would matter if they were read, completed, and turned in. It wouldn't.

The staff on this unit knew Nick and his family well. Nick was the youngest of three boys and was attending middle school when his symptoms began. He was an active and athletic boy, full of energy—not unlike his two older brothers. He always seemed to be full of bruises, but then he was forever running, jumping, climbing and biking. One day at football practice, Nick felt tired and short of breath. The coach had put the team through the paces like any other practice yet Nick had to take a break. When his coach asked if he was all right, he said he had become winded and needed to sit down.

"Maybe you're coming down with something," the coach wondered aloud.

"Maybe," agreed Nick. The coach sent him home.

Sadly, what Nick came down with was not a case of the sniffles or flu that his coach had expected. As the weeks went by, Nick missed more football practices and games than he attended because he felt under the weather. It wasn't until his appetite dwindled and he looked pale that his parents worried his illness might be serious. A doctor appointment and numerous tests later confirmed the diagnosis of leukemia.

Most types of leukemia in the young are quite treatable, but this particular strain of the disease proved difficult to manage. After several rounds of chemotherapy, his blood counts had looked promising. Nick was feeling much better, and after a while, he had been able to return to school full-time. His brothers had breathed a sigh of relief; they needed their pain-in-the-butt brother back! His parents were also overjoyed, but their doctor warned them to be cautiously optimistic as there was always the real threat of relapse.

Six months later, blood work showed all was not well. The cancer had returned. More hospitalizations and more chemotherapy took its toll on Nick and his family. Stronger drugs pushed the disease into remission, and Nick, once again, worked at getting stronger. But only a few months later, the ugly disease came back for a third time, and Nick had a sense of doom— he knew he would not beat it this time. Perhaps his parents and the medical team thought otherwise, but Nick knew. Deep down in his heart, he knew he would have to accept it. He worried about his family. They had thrown everything into helping him beat the horrific disease. Their lives and their bank account had been altered dramatically, and they still had hope. Was it fair for him to give up when those who loved him remained willing to do whatever was necessary to keep him with them?

But Nick was tired. So very tired. Tired of watching his family struggle financially due to his illness. Tired of having at least one of his parents living at Ronald McDonald House at all times, so family life with his brothers was never whole. He was tired of missing his brothers and his friends. He was more than tired of being poked; of toxic chemicals being pumped into him that caused the loss of his hair, his color, his energy, and appetite. He was tired of being too ill to want his favorite food—pizza. He was tired of wondering if he would ever get to drive a car or have a girlfriend. He was tired of wondering what he was missing at school and when he might see the family husky again. He longed to be able to taste food without it being masked by the metallic taste that aggravated the open sores in his mouth.

He thought a great deal about death since his original diagnosis. Most kids his age gave death only a passing thought, but a life threatening illness had a way of making normal teenage issues like prom, Facebook, or birthdays give way to far more philosophical subjects. It weighed on Nick as he wondered if there was life after death. He yearned only to have to worry about making it to football practice on time or how to improve his low English grade.

He was at the beginning of the end of his worries. His decision would not be popular, but he knew he was ready despite not knowing how to help his family understand and comply with his decision. He would start by explaining himself to his favorite nurse.

Chapter 6

As a nurse working on the oncology unit of the hospital, Denise was often required to wear many hats. At times, she was a physical caregiver, a patient advocate, a scientist, a pharmacist, counselor, and sounding board. It was not uncommon to have the same patient readmitted several times, which gave her the opportunity to get to know not only the patient but their family and friends. Such was the case with Nick. She had been assigned to him during each admission which was hospital policy, ensuring some continuity of care. Working on a cancer floor was unique for many reasons. Many of the conversations with her patients were difficult. People having to face the possibility of death were not shy about discussing their hopes, fears, and wishes. So, when Nick asked her to sit beside his bed, she was prepared to have a frank heart-to-heart with him.

Nick made it clear that he was exhausted from

fighting the disease, and he had a sneaking suspicion that the doctors knew there was little more that they could do. He understood their reluctance to be totally honest with his family for fear of taking away all of their hope. Denise sat in the chair with her hands folded in her lap, nodding her head appropriately. She had had this kind of conversation before, but it had been with someone much older, yet no wiser, than the young man before her. He had asked her to listen and assist him with the decision as to what to do next, and she would do her best. Denise explained that the first thing he should do was to have a candid talk with his oncologist to see where his treatment protocol stood. Depending on that discussion's outcome, she would advise bringing in the family's clergy, a social worker and Nick's family. No matter what the prognosis was, it was time for an unavoidable discussion.

Nick's parents were devastated after learning their son was ready to stop treatment and succumb on his own terms. In front of their son, they had kept a brave front, but after leaving his room, they had wept long and hard. They had been confident in the medical team's treatment plan at first, but over the last year, they too had been losing hope. No one knew better than his parents and Denise how much physical suffering and mental anguish the teenager had endured. Everyone on the medical team knew more of the same treatment would not bring them any closer to a cure but would prolong the teen's life for a few months. Nick's parents had heard and listened to the opinions from all involved—most importantly, those of their son. Nick was still a minor, so technically his parents had the final say when it came to his treatment. Nick asked that they allow him to stop his treatment and that they give their consent to his medical team in the morning.

That night while Nick lay in bed, he felt better physically and emotionally than he had for several months. Finally, he had aired everything he had been thinking and feeling. He was choosing the quality of life over quantity. His parents, however, were preparing to make the hardest decision of their lives. It was a lose-lose situation, and they knew it. If they allowed medical treatment to be stopped, they would lose their son sooner than later. If they demanded the treatment continue, not only would they lose their son in a few months anyway, they would risk alienating themselves from him beginning tomorrow. They sat on the gray tweed sofa in the visitor's lounge, holding each other and crying until there were no more tears. The television played quietly in the corner, but neither parent even knew it was on. In a state of pure mental exhaustion, they fell into a fitful sleep.

The crick in her neck and the daylight beginning to peek through the lounge window disturbed Nick's mom from her restless night. She had fallen asleep with her head in her husband's lap, and when she looked up, she saw his head was tilted back, braced against the wall, his eyes still closed. She needed to go down to her son's room to check in on him. As she slowly and quietly hoisted herself off the sofa, she wondered how the beautiful blue bead she held in her hand had been placed there.

Oliver left the sixth floor knowing it wasn't Nick who needed courage. It was his parents. They were fighting a losing battle and were desperate for the peace that accepting their son's decision would bring, ultimately enabling them to let him go.

Chapter 7

The hospital Oliver was in housed thousands of people when the number of patients was added together with the large staff. There were many cries for courage within the institution, and Oliver had a feeling he was supposed to go to the hospital's emergency room. Anticipating an encounter with someone who had been badly injured or very ill, he was surprised to see that the ER was nearly deserted. He stood against a wall not sure what this mission would be about. He looked time and time again at a lady dressed in pink scrubs standing behind the nurses station. Knowing he couldn't be seen, he walked close enough to be able to read her name tag. It said 'Mary RN.'

Oh, she's a nurse, said Oliver to himself. He continued to stand near Mary, learning more about her as if by osmosis. She was on the thin side, standing about five feet six inches tall. Her dark brown, straight, shoulder-length hair matched her dark framed secretary glasses. She wore little makeup and the lipstick she had put on before work was now all over the straw that speared the top of her water cup. Mary sat down on a blue rolling chair and grabbed a metal encased patient chart out of the record carousel. Before she could read or write anything, a patient in a nearby cubicle called out for a nurse. Mary immediately got up and walked toward her patient with Oliver following close behind.

The longer he was near Mary, the more he learned about her. Mary had been a nurse for more than twenty years, ever since she had graduated at the age of twenty-two. She had a good reputation in the ER because she was knowledgeable, caring, and a good co-worker. One day, years earlier, she had slipped on some fluid that had dripped onto the floor during a trauma. She hit the floor—hard. The fall had left her dazed and numb in both legs. The numbness gave way to severe pain, and she was unable to work while she endured month after month of physical therapy and home exercises. The physical rehab would not have been possible without the powerful pain medication she had been prescribed. It took the edge off her pain and enabled Mary to get through each challenging therapy session and be able to sleep at night. Her doctor said she needed to wean off the strong meds to something less addicting. Fear intervened. Mary would not risk feeling the excruciating pain again, so when her doctor cut back her dosage, she found another source of medication; the street. Her pain was kept in check, but now she was considered a drug addict.

Mary had been illegally using drugs for many years, and it haunted her every day. She hated herself for her behavior and how weak she was for letting the drugs run her life. Mary had little self-esteem left and had become bitter about how her life was playing out. She knew she needed to get off the drugs, but she didn't know where to begin, feeling trapped in a way of life she no longer wanted. People close to her had tried to help over the years, but she had lied to them and pushed them away.

Her family needed the good money that Mary had made as a nurse. She was a master at squirreling away small amounts of money and lying about the cost of purchases so her family wouldn't miss the cash she needed to buy her drugs. She had dug herself such a deep hole, and for so many years, she couldn't see a way out.

Mary knew there were plenty of resources right in the hospital where she worked. More than once, she had made her way down to the occupational health office to confide in a health professional and get help, but she had never had the guts to actually enter the office. Instead, each time, she had slinked back to the ER department, hoping no one had spotted her pacing outside the health office's frosted glass door.

Her shift was nearly over for the day, and she was dog-tired. Mary made her way out of the hospital to the bus stop. For once, the bus was on time, and she wearily climbed the steps, showing her bus pass to the driver. Finding a seat alone was not a problem, and she placed her lunch bag next to her. She opened her purse and fumbled around in its dark interior until she felt her worn, faded denim change purse. She flipped the clasp and opened the little bag while keeping it hidden in her purse. She jumped when she saw what was rolling around with the pills—a beautiful, glowing, purple bead—the bead of sobriety. Mary wept. She had no idea who had placed it there, but it was surely a sign. Its presence proved to Mary that not only did someone know of her problem, but they were convinced of her ability to fix it. She snapped closed the change purse. She didn't need a pill now, not ever! Tomorrow she would open that frosted glass door.

Oliver thought his work inside the hospital was finished. But as he left the emergency department, he was directed by an inner spirit to make his way to pediatric surgery on the second floor. Once on the unit, he again took up vigilance beside the nurses station. Two people were at the desk, a nursing assistant and a doctor. When the assistant walked away, Oliver did not feel the need to follow him. In fact, he got the feeling that he should move closer to the doctor. He stood next to the man who was engrossed in a patient's chart that was lengthy and complex. His green scrubs that were covered by a white coat made Oliver think of the operating room. The doctor was a surgeon. The black stitching on the white lab coat said 'Dr. Fred Chambers, Pediatric Thoracic Surgery.' The longer Oliver stood by the man, the more information he learned. Preparations were being made to transplant the heart of a ten-year-old boy into the chest of a seven-year-old girl, and the tales of both children were tragic.

Brandon had been a very active little boy. He was the only boy in the family and was often aggravated by his older and younger sisters. His dirty blonde hair, spray of freckles, and big hazel eyes made him look mischievous, even when he wasn't. His grandfather affectionately called him Opie, a reference to a long-ago beloved television character. Brandon's dad loved the outdoors and most of the recreational activities that went with it. Whatever Brandon's dad liked, Brandon liked. Each season, they enjoyed time together. They fished year round, boated when it was warm, and snowmobiled in the cold. For his last birthday, Brandon had received his very own quad. He loved riding it through the woods, zipping through every mud hole he could find, and then he took pride in washing it back to its original shine. Sometimes his dog, Misty, would sit in the passenger seat, her fur blowing in the wind while Brandon pulled down the brim of his Steelers cap to keep it from blowing off.

The path through the woods was well worn. Brandon had ridden it hundreds of times on his bicycle, and then his little dirt bike, but now the quad was his ride of choice. He knew the trail's every curve, clump of bushes, locations of troublesome rocks and where to watch for deer and ground hogs.

One day after school, Brandon gassed up his quad and headed to the woods with Misty riding shotgun. What Brandon didn't know was that during the night, a large rotted tree had fallen across his riding trail. Coming around the bend, he had no way of anticipating an obstacle on his road. The quad hit the trunk with a loud thud, and both driver and passenger were thrown many yards through the air as the beloved vehicle tumbled over and over into the woods. Misty lay sprawled out in the dirt and leaves. She had landed hard and was dazed but awake. She whimpered a few times, but as the minutes passed, she slowly got up on three of her legs. Her first thought was for her buddy, Brandon. His scent enabled the dog to find the boy quickly. He had been thrown into the woods and was lying very still, bleeding from somewhere on his head while his left leg sat at a peculiar angle. Misty whimpered while she sniffed Brandon's leg. Then she began to bark trying to arouse her best friend. Finally, the dog resorted to licking her master's face and tugging at his clothes, but when nothing woke him up, she trotted back down the trail, limping back to the family home.

Brandon's mom was in the kitchen making

supper, and his dad was tinkering in the garage when Misty approached the house barking furiously. Without looking up from the stove, she commanded, "Stop that barking, Misty!" The barking continued with Misty's nose pressed tight against the screen door. After another minute of relentless noise, Brandon's mom put down her stirring spoon next to the stove and walked to the door.

"Get in here, you," she said none too gently as she opened the door for the pooch. She couldn't help but notice the dog was limping, and her coat was thick with twigs, dirt, and leaves. To her surprise, letting the dog into the house did nothing to quiet her. Misty became more agitated, nose-nudging her adopted mom toward the door. "What on earth is the matter with you?" she asked Misty, squatting down to her level, showing concern. Then it dawned on her that something must be wrong. She had seen Misty jump on the quad with Brandon earlier. If Misty was back so should Brandon. Her heart dropped, and she followed the pet back outside. It was then that she spotted Brandon's helmet sitting in the grass where the quad was usually parked. She began to feel sick.

Chapter 8

The funeral for Brandon was a few days later. He had never regained consciousness and had been put on life support. It took a while for his family to come to terms with his condition, but when testing showed that his head trauma had been so severe that he was brain dead, they had prepared themselves for the unimaginable diagnosis. The young man who had loved to fish would never fish again. His brave parents, determined to see something positive come out of their tragedy, readily agreed to allow Brandon's body to be used to help others. As Brandon lay in his hospital bed waiting to be prepped for surgery, a similar scene was unfolding not far away.

Hope was building in the hospital room of seven-year-old Molly Ann. She had never had the chance to go fishing, to ride her bike through the woods, or do much else that required endurance or physical activity. Her congenital heart condition had been manageable with drugs for the first few years, but as time went on, they were of little use. The only thing that would help now was a new heart, and it was an exciting day when Molly was put on the transplant list. But being on the list was a far cry from getting a heart. The agonizing months of waiting were exhausting for Molly and her parents.

The freckles on Molly's face stood out against her pale skin and her bright red curly hair that sat in a top-knot against the bleached-white hospital pillow. If Brandon was likened to Opie, then Molly could surely be compared to the young orphan Annie! The once exuberant little girl was now reduced to a silent child drifting in and out of consciousness while her sick heart did its best to keep her going.

"Not much longer now," said Oliver to Molly as he stood invisibly by her bedside. Her bright blue eyes fluttered open at the sound of his voice that only she could hear. Her exhausted parents sat at her bedside where they had been stationed since she had been flown in by helicopter the night before. They understood the huge risk that heart transplant surgery meant, but they had no other options. This was their little girl's only chance of survival.

Oliver found his way back to the nurses'

station, once again standing beside the surgeon. He would be chief of the team that would replace Molly's broken heart with Brandon's healthy one. He had assisted with multiple pediatric heart transplants before, but he had never led the team.

There is a first time for everything, Dr. Chambers said to himself. He knew it was true; he had enjoyed success with many personal and professional firsts, but the thought barely calmed his nerves. He was under enormous stress. There was no margin for error. He found some solace knowing he would not have been given the role if senior surgeons were not confident in his abilities. This would be a long surgery involving dozens of health care professionals. The task would take its toll both physically and mentally, and he knew it was imperative that he lead the team with confidence. The text he had just received told him everything was ready, so with a deep breath, he was on his way to the operating room.

Many hours later, Molly Ann was wheeled to pediatric intensive care. The surgery was over and Dr. Chambers, along with his team, had completed the heart transplant. Now it was up to

Molly and her medical team, as he had explained to her parents before walking into the surgeons' locker room. He sat down heavily on the glossy wooden bench that ran in front of his locker. He needed to shower and change out of his sweaty scrubs then remain at the hospital overnight to monitor the progress of his youngest patient and her family. With his tired eyes closed and his head in his hands, he offered up a silent prayer of thanks, followed by a request for a long, healthy life for a beautiful little red-haired girl.

He reached for the crucifix that always hung on a gold chain around his neck. His grandmother had given it to him the day he had graduated from medical school.

"I'm so proud of you, Frederick," she had said to him with her hands cupping his cheeks. "But don't ever think you are a big shot and are doing this alone. You will help people because the Lord guides you to." In one sentence, she had managed to both congratulate him and put him in his place. *Gotta love a grandma from the Bronx,* he smiled to himself.

As he caressed the cross, he felt something else on the chain. Curiosity got the better of him, and he strode to the large mirror above the sinks. His reflection showed that a faintly glowing orange bead was nestled next to the cross. Only Oliver knew how it got there and that it had given the surgeon the confidence and endurance he had needed.

Oliver felt contentment as he walked out of the hospital's front door. It was night now, and the moon and the stars were covered with a thick blanket of clouds. A cool breeze brought the smell and feeling of impending rain. Oliver stepped onto the sidewalk, paused, and closed his eyes while taking a deep breath. He noticed the wind had picked up considerably and was whipping around his head while he felt raindrops sprinkling his face and neck. Opening his eyes, he half expected a heavy downpour to begin, but what he saw made him smile. He was sitting beside his daddy on the Splash Mountain roller coaster, and the rain he had felt had been the water that had been splashed up when their coaster car swished through the stream at the end of the ride. As they came to a stop, Daddy placed his arm around Oliver and gave his shoulder a squeeze.

"You did it, buddy!" said Daddy, smiling, "You were so brave; you did something new!"

Oliver sat up proudly and looked over at his dad.

You can say that again! said Oliver to himself as he felt a mysterious bead in his pants' pocket.

Author

Rosanna Gartley is the mother of four adult children, four bonus adult children and grandmother to 13. A retired nurse practitioner, she currently lives in southwestern Pennsylvania but hails from the Canadian prairies. Rosanna enjoys her family, most things creative and travelling with her husband, John.

Title: Castaway Crown

(Matthew and Anna's Undersea Adventure)

- Author: Rosanna Gartley
- Publisher: MouseGate.com
- Paper Back: ISBN: 9781590953327
- eBook: ISBN: 9781590953358
- Number of pages in the finished book: 64
- Publication Date: April 25, 2017

Matthew and Anna are full of excitement when they learn their family is going on a Disney cruise. With the magic of Disney both children are propelled into an adventure far below the ocean when they are asked to help the sea creatures get rid of a bothersome ghost. With Matthew's above average intellect coupled with Anna's amazing drawing abilities they solve the two-hundred-year old mystery bringing peace to the sea and the ghost.

Beads of Courage®

(Oliver's Story)

- Author: Rosanna Gartley
- Publisher: MouseGate.com.
- Paper Back: ISBN: 9781590952269
- eBook: ISBN: 9781590952320
- Number of pages in the finished book: 64
- Publication Date: April 25, 2017

Baby Oliver's life started out precariously in the neonatal intensive care unit. Each day, while he was a patient, his parents were given beads of various shapes and colors. Each bead symbolized a medical procedure that Oliver had endured on that day. By the time Oliver was discharged, his collection of beads was impressive.

As Oliver grew, his Beads of Courage® continued to hang on his bedroom wall. Not only were they a reminder of what he had lived through but also served as an inspiration for future challenges.

You won't want to miss what happens during a family vacation when this amazing little boy employs Disney magic to help those who need a little courage.